PROSPER'S MOUNTAIN

by Henrietta Branford

Illustrated by Chris Baker

HUTCHINSON

London Sydney Auckland Johannesburg

There was once an old man called Felix. Felix was a gardener – brown from the sun, bent at the knees. When he was young, he wanted a house full of children, but none came.

Most days he rose early, drank a cup of mint tea with his good friend Dorcas, the hen, and strolled under the trees. All day he worked in his garden and in the evening he mended things.

One morning, everything changed.

Felix was in the kitchen making tea when he heard a commotion in the barn. Out he ran, and found Dorcas up on a rafter, cackling fit to bust. Down on the floor, a great big egg was cracking open.

Out rolled a baby boy. He sat up in one half of the egg shell like a prince on his potty, with the other half stuck to his head like a crown.

Felix made him a crib. Dorcas lined it with sheep's wool. They borrowed a goat for milk from the old woman next door. And there they were – as happy as bees in borage.

Where he came from they never found out, but the egg baby made himself at home. He took his milk straight from the goat. He laughed, he played, and his smile lit up the village. Everybody was his friend. Felix and Dorcas named him Prosper, and there was no trouble until his wings began to grow.

'You must be careful now,' said Felix. 'People don't like anybody different.'

He made Prosper a cloak, and showed him how to hide his wings. The cloak was hot and heavy and Prosper didn't want to wear it.

'You must,' said Dorcas. 'Up on the mountain where nobody goes, it will be safe to spread your wings, and feel your two feet leave the ground. Down in the village, never.'

The people in the village were farmers. As long as the wind blew and the rain fell, nobody went hungry. But round about the time that Prosper learned to fly, the weather changed. The wind dropped and the rain stopped. Crops withered on the stalk, and times grew hard.

One night, as Prosper came down off the mountain, the goat woman stopped him. She had been up there too, studying the weather.

'Did you see a strange bird over the mountain?' she asked. 'Only I thought I did. So I wondered.'

'No,' said Prosper. 'I saw no bird.'

But still the goat woman wondered, and the next time Prosper went up, she followed him.

That set the cat among the pigeons. That put the fat in the fire. Because once she'd seen, she had to tell. She told the mayor. He was a rich and powerful man, but all his crops were dying.

'A child with wings,' said he to his wife, 'is not a proper child. It's my belief that child has killed the wind and dried up all the rain.'

'Do you think so?' asked his wife.

'I know so!' said the mayor. And he called a big meeting.

Dorcas hid herself and listened. As soon as she knew what the villagers were planning, she ran home to Felix, and the two of them did some deep talking. They were still talking when a stone flew through the window. They pulled Prosper from his bed and ran out of the back door and away up the mountain.

Night fell as they stumbled up the rocky path, but they did not stop until they'd climbed the first ridge. Looking back, they saw their old home burning. The mayor was there, warming his hands at the blaze, taking what he fancied and throwing the rest to burn.

The goat woman watched, red-faced with shame. What could she do? What could Prosper do, up on the mountain, but watch his home burn?

'We could go down and fight,' he said.

'No,' Felix answered. 'We could not. I'm old. You're young. And Dorcas is a hen.'

Up they went, until the air cut deep, and the cold caught them and squeezed them, and the snow piled a white hill over them, shutting them away from the world. Felix's gnarled hands froze so that he could not open them and Dorcas's red feathers turned to silver. It was a long and bitter night.

In the morning, Prosper climbed out of the snowdrift, took off his cloak, and wrapped it round Felix and Dorcas. Then he flew up until the mountain blazed and dazzled under him.

Towers of green ice shone in the sun and frost fires burned from every jagged peak. Off in the west the storm clouds gathered, fat with snow.

Even as Prosper watched, they boiled and curdled round the mountain peaks, hiding the sun and blotting out the light. Wind ripped the snow from the high tops and sent it streaming like smoke across the sky. The air grew thick and hard as iron.

'That storm will kill us if it finds us on the mountain,' said Prosper. And he flew down to where Felix and Dorcas lay as still as stone.

'Well, my speckled egg,' croaked Dorcas, 'where have you been? What have you seen?'

'I've seen a great storm coming,' said Prosper. 'We must get off the mountain quickly. We must go down to the village and find shelter.'

'We'll find no shelter there,' said Felix. 'We'll die if we go back.'

'We'll die if we don't,' said Prosper.

The path down the mountain was slippery and steep. The wind battered them and the snow blinded them, but Prosper flew on ahead and the old ones followed, trembling with fear of what was waiting in the valley.

The mayor was waiting, with a
stick in his hand and half the
village at his back. 'How dare you show
your face, bird boy?' he shouted. 'We
want no cursed abominations here! You
killed the wind and dried up all the rain!
You, with your wicked wings!'

He tore at Prosper's cloak and raised
his stick high over Prosper's back. The
sky grew dark, the thunder growled, a
flash of lightning stabbed the mountain.
Hard hooves pattered on the dusty road
and the goat woman came running.

'Fool!' she cackled at the mayor. 'Numbskull! Look at the sky!'

The mayor tipped his head back. A gust of wind whipped off his hat and sent it bowling down the road. Fat drops of water plopped onto his face. He dropped his stick and let go of Prosper.

The smell of rain on dust was everywhere. The villagers breathed deeply. Shame filled their hearts for what they'd done – and nearly done.

'What now?' asked Dorcas, helping Prosper to his feet.

'You can stay with me,' said the goat woman, 'until you've built a new house.'

A chink appeared between the storm clouds and the sun peeped through, turning the ice on Prosper's wings to diamonds. Felix picked up the tattered cloak and held it out.

'It was a good cloak, Father,' Prosper said, 'but I don't need it now. I will not wear it any more.'